38
Hig
D1392087

The HAT TRICK

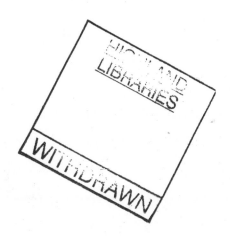

HIGHLAND
LIBRARIES

WITHDRAWN

WITHDRAWN

The HAT TRICK

Terry Deary

HIGH LIFE HIGHLAND	
3800 14 0050573 5	
Askews & Holts	Nov-2014
JF	£5.99

Barrington Stoke

First published in 2002 in Great Britain by
Barrington Stoke Ltd
18 Walker Street, Edinburgh, EH3 7LP

www.barringtonstoke.co.uk

This edition first published 2014

4u2read edition based on *The Hat Trick*,
published by Barrington Stoke in 2000

Text © 2002 Terry Deary
Illustrations © 2014 Martin Remphry

The moral right of Terry Deary and Martin Remphry to be identified
as the author and illustrator of this work has been asserted in
accordance with the Copyright, Designs and Patents Act, 1988

All rights reserved. No part of this publication may be reproduced in
whole or in any part in any form without the written permission of
the publisher

A CIP catalogue record for this book is available
from the British Library upon request

ISBN: 978-1-78112-415-4

Printed in China by Leo

Contents

1   Magic Hat Trick   1

2   Rubbing Dubbin   9

3   Redby Rivals   14

4   Mud and Blood   22

5   Barged and Beaten   29

6   Goals and Glory   33

7   Magic and Memories   43

Chapter 1
Magic Hat Trick

The great thing about football is the memories it gives you. I've seen exciting matches that I'll remember for the rest of my life ... even if I live to be 137!

But there's one match I'll remember till I'm 237. It's the one I played in over 60 years ago, on Boxing Day. It was the only time in my life that I ever scored three goals.

It was my dad that got me into football. "I could have played for England, Jud!" he told me as we kicked the ball from one end of our little back garden to the other.

"Why didn't you, Dad?"

"I was too busy winning the war," he said.

When I was little, I thought Dad was a hero with a gun! As I grew older, I found out he was only a cook at the army camp.

But when I was much older, I understood why he said, "We all played our part to help win the war. It's just like football. The goalie at the back is just as important as the players up front who shoot all the goals."

He kicked the ball hard and it flew past my ear and into the hedge. "Dad 10 – Jud 1!" he said and went inside for a cup of tea.

Most times he beat me 10–1 … if he didn't beat me 10–0. But I didn't mind. He wasn't one

of those dads who was soft and let his kid win.
I learned more that way.

And that Christmas Eve I lost by only 10–2!

That was the Christmas I'll never forget.
We had Christmas lunch, then we sat by the
Christmas tree to open our presents. I tried
to look as if I liked the jumpers and the books
and the games and chocolates … but there was
nothing exciting. And no toys this year.

"You're getting a bit old for toys," Mum said. "So now your dad can't buy them for you and play with them himself."

Gran sat in the corner and grinned. The year before, Dad had got me a train set, then spent the next two days playing with it!

"No, Mum," I said with a sigh.

"Here, Jud!" Dad cried. "I wonder what's in the magic hat?"

"Ohhhh! The magic hat!" I said.

Gran smiled and she gazed into the fire. She knew what Dad was going to do next.

Dad knew a few magic tricks from his time in the army. He used to do them for me on my birthday. He did a magic act for my friends. At the end he always pulled a present from his top hat. But he'd never done this trick at Christmas before.

He went to get his hat. I had no idea what would come out. Each time he did this trick I got so excited that I didn't look to see how he did it. When I asked him, he would just say, "It's magic!"

"Say the magic words, Jud!" he boomed now.

"Abracadabra, hocus-pocus!" I said.

He pulled a parcel from the empty hat. He did! I know he did!

I ripped the paper off and held the present in my hands as if it were made of gold.

"Boots!" I said and my eyes filled with tears. "Football boots!" I said over and over again. I was trying not to cry. Dad was trying hard not to sniff too. Mum was trying hard not to smile.

"Thanks, Dad," I said.

"And your mum," Dad said.

"Thanks, Mum."

"Dad spoils you," she said.

Chapter 2
Rubbing Dubbin

I wanted to put them on at once and run out and play. But Dad said, "Football boots are made of leather. They'll crack if you get them wet."

It was true. In those days, boots were made of plain, brown leather with a heavy toe-cap.

"What do I do, Dad?"

"You rub stuff called dubbin into them," he said. "It makes the leather soft and stops it cracking. We'll do it now and then you can wear the boots tomorrow."

"Have you got any dubbin?" I asked.

"Under the kitchen sink," he said.

For an hour we rubbed the smelly dubbin all over the boots. We rubbed them till they were warm.

"That helps the dubbin soak in," Dad told me.

The boots sat under the Christmas tree and shone. They were the best present I'd had so far. In fact, they were the best I'll ever have, even if I live to be 337.

"They're magic," Dad said.

"Get off," I laughed.

But Dad wasn't laughing.

"These boots have a magical mind of their own," he said.

"They haven't!" I told him, but I wasn't so sure.

"Paid extra for the magic, I did," Dad went on. "You'll see."

"When? When can I try them, Dad?"

"Tomorrow in the park, Jud. I'll take you down there and you can try them out."

That was it. That was the end of my Christmas. All I wanted was for tomorrow to come. I hardly slept at all that night. I couldn't wait for the morning.

I couldn't wait for the fun to start. But I didn't know just how much fun I was going to have.

Chapter 3
Redby Rivals

I shook Dad awake at 6 o'clock the next morning. He told me to go away. He wasn't very polite.

At 7 o'clock, I took him a cup of tea.

"These are the only two days I get off till Easter," he told me crossly. "I'm back in the shop tomorrow."

"Yes, Dad. Can I try the boots on now, Dad?"

"You can, but don't make a sound or your mum will be after you."

"No, Dad," I said and rushed down to the living room.

I put the boots on over my short white socks. They were a snug fit.

I stood on the living-room floor kicking a ball around that wasn't even there. The fire was the goal. *Foof!* The shot had gone in. *Wahhhh!* In my mind, the crowd went wild.

At 9 o'clock, Dad came down. He had his coat and scarf on.

It was grey and chilly outside, but I wore my white shorts and a green jumper.

"OK, Jud! Come on over to the park and I'll show you how Stanley Matthews won the 1953 Cup Final for Blackpool."

A fine mist blew in off the sea. There was no one about. Dad made me wear my shoes for the walk to the sea and on to the park.

"You'll wear your studs out on the pavement," he told me.

I tied the boot laces together and slung them over my shoulder. It was only a ten-minute walk to the sea. The water looked as dead and grey as the sky. The park was not far away. There was some life there. Two groups of boys were changing into football strips on one of the park's pitches.

I knew the strips at once. The black-and-white ones were Redby Junior School, our enemies in everything. The green-and-white ones were Seaburn Junior School. Our school.

I forgot about my kick-about with Dad. This was a real match. I was too shy to try my boots out in front of them.

Dad looked at me. "What's the matter, Jud?"

"They're top class, Dad!" I said.

"How do you know?" he asked. "You haven't seen them play."

"No! I mean they're the top class. The boys at the top of our school. A whole year above me."

"So why are they playing on Boxing Day? Where's their teacher? Who's the ref?"

"I don't know, Dad."

"Then let's ask them, shall we?"

I blushed all over. My face was hot. But Dad chose not to see. "Hey, lads!"

A big boy with fair hair frowned at Dad. It was Larry Potts, the captain.

"What do you want?" snapped Larry.

"Is this a proper match?" asked Dad.

Larry stuck his fists on his hips. "The league match was a draw last month. This is the replay."

"Want a ref?"

Larry Potts looked at the Redby captain, who nodded.

"Then I'm your man," Dad said and trotted smiling into the centre circle. He left me to shiver alone on the touchline, still hot in the face.

I knew, there and then, that I would never forgive my dad, not if I lived to be 437.

But that was before I knew why the boots were magic.

Chapter 4
Mud and Blood

"You have to have a goalie," Dad said to our captain, before the game started.

Larry Potts frowned at him. "Stevie Mann is our goalie. But he's gone away for Christmas."

"Then you'll have to put someone else in goal!" Dad told him.

The Seaburn players looked away from their captain or at the ground. No one wanted the job.

Dad pointed at me. "Then let our Jud go in goal for you," he said.

The team looked at me with scorn. "A little third year!" Jimmy Archer said with a smile.

Larry Potts frowned at him. "You go in goal, then!" he said.

"Nah!" Jimmy spat. "Let the kid go in goal. Better than nothing."

"It's not allowed in the league rules," said the Redby captain. His name was Alan Bourne. Just then I hated him.

"But this isn't a league match," I shouted.

"Yeah!" Larry Potts agreed. "Are you scared of letting the kid go in goal in case you get beat?"

"No! I'm scared in case the kid gets hurt."

"Look," Dad butted in. "I'm Jud's dad. I'll take the blame if something goes wrong."

Alan Bourne didn't look happy, but he said, "Let's get on with it, then."

I had my new green jumper on so I was perfect for the goal. Well, I may have been a bit small. I couldn't even jump up and touch the crossbar.

"Better than nothing, I suppose," said Jimmy Archer.

So I was playing in the team with all my heroes.

The field was muddy and the ball kept sticking. There were a lot of sliding tackles. Studs crunched as they hit shin pads. It wasn't pretty to watch but it was exciting.

I cheered like a fan every time we moved up the pitch. Then I shivered when the Redby players came my way with the ball.

Then Alan got the ball past Larry. Larry made a sharp turn and his right leg stuck in the mud. He fell with a cry of pain. He had twisted his leg. Alan jumped over Larry's body and raced for my goal. He got as far as the edge of the penalty area.

I did everything my dad had always told me to do. I rushed out to narrow the angles. I spread myself as wide as my skinny body would let me. There was no way past to my left or right!

Then Alan chipped the ball over my head. I turned and rushed back to my goal line to try and make a save. I saw the muddy leather ball smack onto the crossbar and bounce out. Before I could get out of the way, the ball hit me smack in the face. I felt the blood gush

from my nose. The ball bounced back into my goal. Redby 1 – Seaburn 0.

I wanted to sink into the ground.

Redby went wild. I wiped the blood off my face onto the sleeve of my jumper.

"Bad luck, Jud," our winger said as he took the ball from me.

"Sorry," I said. "Blame me."

"One of those things," he said. He smiled and gave me a wink. "Everything to play for now!"

That cheered me up. But not for long.

Chapter 5
Barged and Beaten

Larry Potts was limping around in the middle of the pitch. The other side could get past him now. But for a long while there was someone else there to stop them ... Me.

I was small and fast. I dived to tip hard shots round the post. I waded into the mud to take the ball off the Redby forwards. I got to all the cross shots too.

My team were looking at me with a new kind of respect. I loved it. Even my dad looked pleased.

As Alan got clear and ran towards me, I knew I could stop whatever he fired at me. He seemed to know it too. In a panic, he kicked the ball far too soon. It slammed into my chest and I held it tight and safe.

But Alan didn't stop running. He raced on. I turned sideways to meet him. He met my shoulder with his shoulder and I sailed over my goal line, still holding the ball.

Alan turned away and hit the air.

"Come on, Ref!" Charlie Carter said with a groan. "That's not fair! He's twice the size of Jud!"

This time Dad was no help. "Fair shoulder charge. Nothing in the rules says the players

have to be the same size. The goal stands.
Redby 2 – Seaburn 0."

Dad looked at his watch, placed two fingers
to his lips and blew. "Half-time! Change ends!"

Our team was not happy as it drifted down to the far end of the pitch to start the second half. Larry Potts stood there with us all around him. "They're going to hammer Jud in goal, now they've got away with it once," he said.

"I'll be ready for them next time," I said.

Larry shook his head. "I'm to blame. I can't do a thing with my leg this bad. I think it would be best if I went in goal from now on. Charlie, drop back to cover in the centre of defence."

"What about me?" I asked in a small voice.

"Take Charlie's place at centre forward. Hang around in the middle and make a pest of yourself," Larry told me.

"Centre forward!" I'll swear I felt those magic boots tingle when I said it.

This was the chance my boots had been waiting for!

Chapter 6
Goals and Glory

We both looked daft. My green jumper was much too small for Larry and his shirt hung round me like a tent. But I didn't care how I looked. I was happy.

Larry was brave. He stood on his bad leg and lashed at the ball with the other. His face was pale and I could tell it hurt. But his kicks from our goal went as far as the centre circle.

Charlie ran up to me. "Hang around the centre spot, Jud. When the ball lands just push it forward for Dave Small to run on to."

I nodded. I knew what he was saying. But it didn't work out that way and I blame the boots.

Larry sent the next kick high into the air. I was under it. It bounced and I put a foot out to push it on to Dave. But the ball bounced higher than I thought. I got my foot under it but that only sent it high into the air again.

The Redby goalie was standing on the edge of his penalty box. He watched in horror as the ball landed behind him on the penalty spot, bounced once and flew between the posts.

Dad blew. "Goal! Redby 2 – Seaburn 1!" he shouted.

Charlie Carter shook his head. "Not quite what I meant, Jud ... but not bad!"

"Thanks, Charlie," I said. It was hard to speak at all.

The game got harder after that. I was no longer a joke. Seaburn, cheered on by my goal, pressed forward in attack after attack. I spent more and more time in the Redby penalty area. But their goalie was on form.

I suppose you could call my second goal a bit of an odd one too. Charlie Carter pushed the ball forward to me on the edge of the penalty area. All I could see was a wall of three or four black-and-white striped shirts.

"Cross it!" Jim Archer called from the far side of the box.

Dad was a good teacher. I got my toe-cap under the ball and lifted it clear over the heads of the other side. Their goalie ran out ... his hands would get to the ball before Jim's head did.

Then a sudden gust of wind made the ball swerve in the air. The goalie tried to turn back, but he slipped in the mud. He was flat on his back when the ball drifted under the crossbar and over the line.

"Goal! Redby 2 – Seaburn 2!" Dad called. "Five minutes to play."

There were green-and-white shirts all round me. They slapped my back till it was sore.

"Go for the hat trick, Jud," Dave Small told me. "You can do it."

But the time went by and it was Redby who went forward. Larry in goal stopped a shot with his bad knee. With one last painful kick he sent the ball upfield. I was standing in the centre circle. I let it pass me, then I set off to chase it.

What happened next was weird. I'll never understand it even if I live to be 537.

It was as if the other 21 players on the pitch were hardly moving and I was the only one running at full speed. And, as I ran, there was silence all round me. The world stood still as I raced forward.

Maybe the other team were waiting for me to pass the ball. Maybe they were waiting for me to trip up. Maybe everyone was waiting for someone else to stop me ... or maybe the boots were doing their magic.

My first kick took me past a defender who just stood there. My second took me past the full-back, who seemed stuck in the mud. Then there was only the goalie to beat. He spread his arms and legs out wide so I couldn't see any of the goal.

My right foot went back to kick the ball as hard as I could. That would have been a mistake. But the boots took over. My foot hit the ground hard and skidded, so my toe-cap sent the ball forward.

There was only one way I was going to score, that was through their goalie's legs ... and that's where the magic boots put the ball!

As the ball crossed the line Dad blew for the end of the game. "Goal and full-time! Redby 2 – Seaburn 3!"

I could have exploded I was so happy and Dad was almost the same. One by one, my team-mates shook my hand. It was their turn to be shy now. Even the Redby team lined up to say, "Well done!"

I swapped shirts with Larry.

"Play next week, Jud?" he asked.

I shook my head. "No. You know the league won't allow it."

He nodded. "They may change the rules one day."

"One day," I said.

Chapter 7
Magic and Memories

Dad and I crept in by the kitchen door.

"Put your boots in the oven for a minute to dry out, then the mud will just drop off," Dad told me.

But as we tried to creep up the stairs to change, Mum heard us. She opened the living-room door and went mad.

"What have you done to your green jumper? Look at it! And look at your face! The blood on your nose. What have you been up to?"

"Playing football," I said in a soft voice.

"You will never, ever play football again!" she said and I knew she meant it. "Hockey, netball or tennis, that's what girls play. Football's not a game for girls and it never will be!"

"Our Jud had a great time," Dad said.

"And that's another thing," Mum said, very angry. "You can stop calling her 'Jud'. Her name is Judith."

"Yes, love," Dad said. He knew when he had lost.

Then we got a long talk on why it was wrong for girls to play football. In the end, Mum turned to Gran. "What do you say, Gran?" she asked.

"I say … What's that horrid smell? Have you left something in the oven?"

"The magic boots!" Dad and I yelled and rushed into the kitchen to get them.

It was too late. They were burnt. I never wore them again, so I never knew if it was their magic or Dad's training that got me that hat trick.

Those three magic goals. The one hat trick of my life.

"Good thing too," said Mum with a sniff. "I'll go out and buy you hockey boots in the sales."

I don't blame Mum. Sixty years ago, girls didn't play football. But it's not like that now, I'm glad to say.

I forgive her. You see, Mum could stop me playing football. But she could never, ever take away the magic memories of that day.

The great thing about football is the memories it gives you. And I'll remember my hat trick if I live to be 637!

Our books are tested
for children and young people by
children and young people.

Thanks to everyone who consulted on
a manuscript for their time and effort in
helping us to make our books better
for our readers.

More *4u2read* titles ...

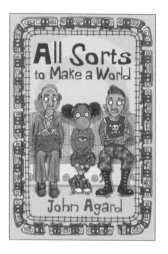

All Sorts to Make a World
JOHN AGARD

Shona's day has been packed with characters.

Now Shona and her dad are on a Tube train that's stuck in a tunnel and everyone is going ... bananas!

Deadly Letter
MARY HOFFMAN

Prity wants to play with the other children at school, but it's hard when you're the new girl and you don't know the rules. And it doesn't help when you're saddled with a name that sounds like a joke.

Will Prity ever fit in?

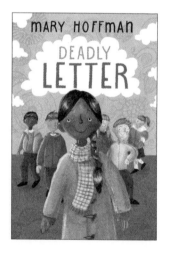

Nadine Dreams of Home
BERNARD ASHLEY

Nadine finds Britain scary. Not scary like soldiers, or the sound of guns. But scary in other ways. If only her father were here. But it's just Nadine, her mother and her little brother now. They have no friends, no English, and no idea if they will ever see Nadine's father again. But then Nadine finds a special picture, and dreams a special dream ...

Mozart's Banana
GILLIAN CROSS

No one can tame Mozart's Banana. Even Sammy Foster failed, and he reckons he's the boss of the school. Mozart's Banana is just too crazy.

But then Alice Brett turns up. Alice is as cool as a choc-ice, and she isn't going to let anyone get the better of her, horse or boy ...

www.barringtonstoke.co.uk

More *4u2read* titles ...

How Brave Is That?
ANNE FINE

Tom's a brave lad. All he's ever wanted to do is work hard at school, pass his exams and join the army. He never gives up, even when terrible triplets turn his life upside down at home. But when disaster strikes on exam day, Tom has to come up with a plan. Fast. And it will be the bravest thing he has ever done!

The Haunting of Uncle Ron
ANNE FINE

Ian thinks the new girl next door looks amazing. But he's not so keen on Uncle Ron, the world's most boring visitor.

Ian can't stand it a moment longer. He must get rid of Uncle Ron. What Ian needs is a plan – and perhaps a helper ...

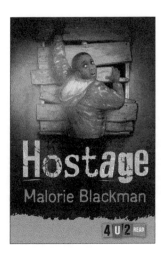

Hostage
MALORIE BLACKMAN

"I'll make sure your dad never sees you again!"

Blindfolded. Alone. Angela has no idea where she is or what will happen next. The only thing she knows is she's been kidnapped. Is she brave enough to escape?

Wartman
MICHAEL MORPURGO

Dilly's life was great till he got a wart on his knee.

Now everyone stares and calls him 'Wartman'.

How can Dilly get rid of the wart and get his life back on track?

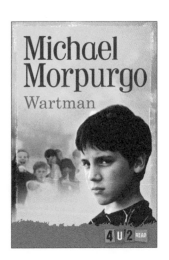

www.barringtonstoke.co.uk